DETROIT PUBLIC LIBRARY
3 5674 00639053 9

D1292384

Benjy
in
Business

Other Books by Jean Van Leeuwen

I Was a 98-Pound Duckling
Too Hot for Ice Cream
The Great Christmas Kidnaping Caper
Seems Like This Road Goes On Forever
Tales of Oliver Pig
More Tales of Oliver Pig
The Great Rescue Operation
Amanda Pig and Her Big Brother Oliver
Benjy and the Power of Zingies
Tales of Amanda Pig

ODD JOBS MAN
weeding $2.00 walk dogs 35¢
picking up sticks 50¢ sweeping $1.00
cleaning rooms 40¢ water plants 40¢
pick up rocks 50¢
Benjy Wilkins 641-2250
helper Jason McFeely 641-7690
Thank You

BENJY IN BUSINESS

Jean Van Leeuwen

pictures by Margot Apple

DIAL BOOKS FOR YOUNG READERS

E. P. Dutton, Inc. NEW YORK

Published by
Dial Books for Young Readers
A Division of E. P. Dutton, Inc.
2 Park Avenue
New York, New York 10016

Design by Susan Lu
Printed in the U.S.A.
First Edition
(COBE)
10 9 8 7 6 5 4 3 2 1

Library of Congress Cataloging in Publication Data
Van Leeuwen, Jean. Benjy in business.
Summary: Eight-year-old Benjy tries various schemes
to earn money to buy a baseball glove.
[1. Moneymaking projects—Fiction.]
I. Apple, Margot, ill. II. Title.
PZ7.V3273Ben 1983 [Fic] 82-22158
ISBN 0-8037-0865-3
ISBN 0-8037-0873-4 (lib. bdg.)

For David,

ODD-JOBS MAN,

USED-TOY SALESMAN,

AND ENTREPRENEUR

J.V.L.

1

»»»»»»»»»»»»»»

Benjy was in the discount store when he saw it.

His mother had just piled a leaning tower of disposable-diaper boxes into the shopping cart and was moving on to the toothpaste, shampoo, and headache-remedy department. From the length of her shopping list it looked like she was going to be there a long time.

"Can I go look around?" asked Benjy.

His mother didn't answer. She was too busy watching the baby. Benjy's sister had this game she played where she reached into the cart from her seat on top and threw things out as her mother put them in. Then she laughed like crazy. Benjy's mother looked like she needed a headache remedy already.

"Can I, Mom?" Benjy asked again.

His mother's eyes finally focused on him. "Okay," she said. "But meet us at the register in ten minutes."

"Sure," said Benjy.

First he made a quick tour of the shoe department to see what kind of sneakers they had. Boring plain white or baby Mickey Mouse was all. No blue lightning stripes or cleats on the bottom like the ball players wore. He wasn't going to be able to hit his mother for new sneakers today.

Benjy moved on to the toy department. He had just enough allowance money to buy one pack of baseball cards. He took ten packs off the rack and tried to figure out which one had his favorite player, Clyde Johnson, inside. This was hard to do, because out of forty-eight cards in a pack, only three pictures showed. And the three that showed were never the guys you wanted. Benjy held up each pack to the light and tried to peer in the sides. But it didn't work. He figured this was what the baseball-card makers counted on. You never got the players you wanted, so you kept buying. If only he had X-ray vision, he could put the baseball-card makers out of business.

After a while he noticed that the salesclerk, a skinny, pimply kid, was giving him the evil eye. Also he'd just about used up his ten minutes, and he still had another stop to make. Benjy put back all the other packs and kept the one with Marty Fox's picture showing. Marty Fox was his second favorite player and he didn't have him this year.

Then he went to check out the sporting goods department.

That was where he saw it.

It was a beautiful newest-model super-deluxe Clyde Johnson fielder's mitt. The leather was soft and smooth and just the right color of reddish brown. It had fancy lacing and a perfect pocket, the kind that a ball would fall right into and stay there. And it had Clyde Johnson's signature, big, black, and bold, written right across the pocket. Clyde Johnson, the top home-run hitter and best centerfielder in the American League.

With a mitt like that Benjy could make stupendous catches up against the centerfield wall, just like Clyde Johnson. He knew he could. He'd leap high in the air and the ball would be drawn into his mitt as if by a magnet. And it would stay there, in that perfect pocket. He'd never drop the ball again if he had that mitt.

He had to have it.

Benjy took the mitt down from the shelf. He smelled the genuine leather smell and ran his finger over the Clyde Johnson signature. He slipped it on his left hand. It felt terrific, like he was ready for the major leagues.

There was a ticket hanging from the lacing. Benjy looked at it. "$22.95," it said. He hurried to find his mother.

She was at the cash register, unloading things from the shopping cart onto the checkout counter. His sister was helping. As Benjy approached he saw the baby pick up a package of paper plates and toss them toward the cashier. The plates sailed over the cashier's head and landed on top of a pile of money in the next register.

Not bad. The kid had a great arm. The Yankees ought to sign her up.

"Oh, Melissa!" cried Benjy's mother, running to retrieve the plates. She looked like she was in need not only of a headache remedy but of a cure for acid indigestion as well.

Benjy thought maybe this wasn't the best moment to ask her to buy him the mitt.

But he had to have it.

42

He stuck the hand with the mitt on it behind his back. With his other hand he helped his mother finish unloading the cart. She smiled at him. It was kind of a weak smile, but it was something.

"Mom," he said, smiling back, "you'll never guess what I found. It's really fantastic, Mom."

"Let me guess," said his mother wearily. Her smile faded fast, he noticed. "It's either sneakers so amazing that when you put them on you travel at the speed of light, or a bat that hits a baseball a mile."

Not bad guesses, he had to admit. His mother knew him like a book.

"Close," he said. And he brought out his left hand from behind his back.

She looked at it. Only something was wrong. He could tell by her expression that she wasn't seeing the just-right leather and the perfect pocket and the real genuine signature of Clyde Johnson. He could tell that she didn't really understand what having a mitt like that would do for his baseball career.

"You already have a mitt," she said.

"But, Mom," said Benjy. "It's so old. The leather's cracked and the pocket's no good." She had bought it for him at a garage sale about two years ago. It was so old that the player whose signature was on it didn't even play anymore. Benjy saw him doing grass seed commercials on TV.

"Just because it's old," his mother said, "doesn't mean it's no good."

He knew she would say that. Somehow he had to make her understand. But how could he explain the magic of having a mitt with Clyde Johnson's signature on it? It was like Clyde Johnson would be there with him, helping him make stupendous catches. Like his greatness would rub off and make Benjy great too.

Benjy showed his mother the soft leather and the perfect pocket. He pointed out the signature. "This is a Clyde Johnson mitt," he said. "It's the best."

Finally she seemed to grasp what he was saying.

"You really feel you need it, don't you?" she said.

Benjy nodded. It looked like he had her.

"And what's the price of this magical mitt?"

Benjy checked the ticket again. "It's only twenty-two ninety-five."

"Twenty-two ninety-five?" she repeated. "Twenty-two dollars and ninety-five cents?"

Uh-oh. He could see by her frown that he'd had a setback. Probably she thought mitts cost about $3.98.

His mother was shaking her head. "I'm sorry,

Benjy," she said. "But that's too much. I've just spent my last twenty-two ninety-five to keep your sister in diapers. But I'll tell you what. Why don't you put it on your birthday list?"

It wasn't fair. If she could spend $22.95 on his sister, why couldn't she spend $22.95 on him? He couldn't help it that he didn't wear diapers. And besides that, his birthday wasn't until September, two whole months away.

"But, Mom," he said, "I can't wait for my birthday. Baseball season will be practically over by then."

"Don't you have any money saved?" she asked.

He shook his head. He knew what was in his monkey bank at home. About twenty cents.

"Well, then," she said, "maybe you'll have to start saving."

"But, Mom," Benjy began again.

His mother gave him her look that said he'd just run into a stone wall. "No more 'But, Mom's,' " she said. "It's time to go home, Benjy. You'll have to put it back."

The bags with her purchases were all packed up ready to go in the shopping cart. In another minute the baby would start unpacking them.

Benjy knew when he was beaten.

He walked slowly back to the sporting goods

department. He ran his hand one last time over the mitt's smooth leather and punched his fist into the perfect pocket. Then he put it as high up on the shelf as he could reach so no one else would see it and buy it.

"I'll be back," he told Clyde Johnson under his breath.

He would be back. He had to have that mitt. And before the end of baseball season too.

2

»»»»»»»»»»»»»»

On the way home in the car Benjy did a few calculations.

If he saved his entire allowance of fifty cents a week, every single week, it would take forty-six weeks to save up enough money for the mitt. Forty-six weeks—that was practically a year. That was worse than waiting till his birthday. And he could never buy baseball cards or bubble gum all that time, either.

That was no good. Where else could he get some money?

Sometimes on holidays his Aunt Ruthie sent him

a card with a dollar inside. Only there weren't any holidays coming up soon. The Fourth of July was already past. The next holiday was Labor Day. He tried to remember if she ever sent him a Labor Day card. He didn't think so. Anyway, he couldn't wait till Labor Day. The summer would be over.

What if he wrote to Aunt Ruthie and told her it was an emergency and asked her to advance the five dollars she always sent him for his birthday? But he had a feeling his mother wouldn't like that. And besides, he'd still have a long way to go to get to $22.95.

There was only one thing to do. He would have to get a job. Part-time, of course, so he'd still have time to play baseball.

"Mom," he said, "what kind of job do you think I could get?"

"Job?" said his mother.

"For the summer. To make money. To buy the mitt," he said.

"Ah," said his mother. "You're serious about this project, I see."

Benjy nodded.

"Well," she said, "I don't know. Summer jobs are hard to find, even for teenagers. It might be pretty tough for an eight-year-old."

"I'm eight and three quarters," said Benjy.

"Or for an eight-and-three-quarters-year-old," said his mother.

Benjy thought about all the kids he knew who had jobs. There was his friend Danny's brother. He delivered newspapers. But you had to be ten or eleven to do that. Besides, you had to get up at five o'clock every morning. Benjy could barely make it at seven thirty. There was Charlie Fryhoffer across the street who mowed lawns. But Benjy's father wouldn't even let him touch their electric mower. Some other kids baby-sat. But his parents still got a sitter for him when they went out. There were boys who worked in the grocery store and the gas station. But you had to be older for that too. Every single job he could think of was for older kids.

"There's got to be something," said Benjy. "I'm very strong. Maybe I could get a job at the garden store lifting fertilizer bags."

His mother nodded. "Or at the brickyard lifting concrete blocks. Or maybe moving pianos."

Benjy looked at her. Somehow he had the idea she was pulling his leg. She never took him seriously, that was her problem. He would show her. He'd look in the newspaper when he got home, at the want ads. He'd find his own job.

The minute they got home, Benjy's mother disappeared into the kitchen. He heard the refrigerator door open and close. Then he heard the baby's squeal of protest as she caught sight of one of those disgusting orange and green baby dinners. "Now, Melissa," said his mother's voice. "It's yum-yum." His sister was no dummy. She didn't fall for that kind of talk. "Gork!" she yelled at the top of her lungs, pounding on her tray.

That would take care of his mother for a while. Benjy spread out the newspaper on the living room floor and opened it to the ad section. Then he lay down next to it, a marker in his hand. That was the way his mother did it when she was looking for garage sales.

HELP WANTED, said the heading at the top of the page. And underneath it were bunches and bunches of ads. This looked promising. What did his mother mean, there weren't many summer jobs?

He looked through them. He could see right away that a lot of them weren't right for him: Hairdresser, Nurse for Night Shift, Computer Programmer, Receptionist for Dental Office. And some that sounded pretty good were definitely for grown-ups. Like: Bus Driver, Coach for Junior High Sports Program, and Auto Mechanic. Still, when he finished looking, he had four jobs circled: Delivery Boy for Drugstore, Dishwasher, Pizza Cook, and Tree Man.

That was better than he'd hoped for. Four jobs to choose from. And two of them even sounded like fun. He could just see himself climbing high into a giant oak tree, his trusty ax in his hand. Or then again he could see himself in the pizza store, popping a delicious sausage and pepperoni pizza into the oven with one hand while he munched on a slice with the other.

Which would he rather be—a tree man or a pizza man? All in all, being a tree man would be more exciting. He'd get to swing by ropes and wear shoes with special cleats for climbing, and he'd really build up his arm muscles with all that chopping. And it would be dangerous too. His mother would worry every day about a tree falling on him.

Benjy took the newspaper with him to the telephone. He started to dial the number of the tree company. Then he noticed something in fine print at the bottom of the ad. DRIVER'S LICENSE REQUIRED.

He put the phone down. It looked like he was going to have to wait awhile to be a tree man. Oh, well, his mother probably wouldn't have let him do it, anyway.

He picked up the phone again and dialed the number of the pizza restaurant.

A man answered. "Anthony's Pizza."

What were you supposed to say when you applied for a job, anyway? His friend Jason would know. He was always good at talking to grown-ups. But Jason wasn't here.

Benjy tried to make his voice sound as grown-up as possible. "I—I'm calling about the job in the paper," he said.

"Jobspilled," said the man. He sounded like he had a mouthful of pizza. Benjy couldn't understand him.

"What did you say?" asked Benjy.

"Jobspilled," said the man, louder. "Get it? Filled." And he hung up.

That took care of two jobs in less than two minutes. Benjy looked again at the ads. Which should he be—a delivery boy or a dishwasher? If he was a delivery boy, at least he could ride his bike. He'd be outside. He dialed the number at the bottom of the ad.

"Phillips Pharmacy," said a woman's voice.

"I'm calling about the job in the paper," said Benjy. "Delivery boy."

"Oh, yes," said the woman. She sounded friendly. "We need a boy with a bicycle to make deliveries. Prescriptions, you know. Just in the afternoons, from one to five."

So far so good. The hours were perfect. He'd still have time to play baseball.

"Would you be interested in coming in to see Mr. Phillips?"

"Yes," said Benjy. "Please."

"Fine," said the woman. "Now, you know where we are, don't you? It's the corner of Park and Hillview. On the north side of Ridgewood Road."

Ridgewood Road. His mother wouldn't let him cross Ridgewood Road on his bike. Not until he was twelve, at least. Too much traffic.

"Uh—thanks," said Benjy. "But I guess I'm not interested. But thanks."

He hung up. There wasn't any choice left. He was going to have to be a dishwasher. If that job wasn't filled already too. He could see himself up to his elbows in soapsuds all day long. Washing dishes wasn't exactly top on his list of things he liked to do. In fact it was way down there at the bottom. But it would be worth it if he could earn the money to buy that Clyde Johnson mitt.

The ad said to ask for Mr. Barker. Benjy did. It was beginning to come back to him now how Jason talked to grown-ups on the phone to make himself sound older. He used his deepest voice and all the big words he could think of.

"Mr. Barker," he said, "I'm calling about the job of dishwasher that was advertised in today's newspaper."

"Sure, kid," said Mr. Barker.

Well, at least he hadn't hung up the phone.

"Is the position still available?" asked Benjy.

"Sure is," said Mr. Barker. "It's hard work, but the pay is fair and the place is clean. If you're interested, come in and see me."

"I'll do that," said Benjy.

"There's just one thing," said Mr. Barker. "How old are you?"

Benjy swallowed hard. "Eight," he said in a low voice.

"Eighteen?" said Mr. Barker.

Benjy hesitated. It didn't matter. He'd know when he saw him anyway.

"Eight," said Benjy. "And three quarters."

"Oh," said Mr. Barker. There was a long pause on the phone. Then he said, "I'm sorry, kid, but eight and three quarters is too young for this job.

There's a lot of pots and pans, a lot of heavy lifting. You know what I mean."

"I'm very strong," said Benjy.

"Yeah," said Mr. Barker. "I'm sure you are. Tell you what, you come back and see me in five or six years. Then I'll put you to work. Okay?"

Five or six years! He couldn't get a job for five or six years. This was getting worse and worse. He'd be too old to play baseball before he could get his mitt.

"Okay," Benjy mumbled. He forgot about using his deepest voice and his biggest words. "So long, Mr. Barker. Thanks anyway."

And he hung up the phone.

3

›››››››››››››

"I hear you're looking for work," said Benjy's father at the dinner table.

Benjy nodded glumly.

"Any prospects?" asked his father.

"Not for five or six years," said Benjy.

"Eight is kind of young to get a job," said his father.

"Eight and three quarters," said Benjy. "The thing is, I can't wait. I need the money now. I've got to get that mitt before baseball season is over."

Benjy's father nodded. "I know the feeling," he said. "All too well. It has struck me on several occasions. I remember a certain fishing pole in a store window when I was about ten."

"And a red sports car," said Benjy's mother, "just last month."

"What did you do?" asked Benjy. He was always surprised to find out that his father used to like things like fishing and baseball. Now all he did was work and watch TV and fool around in his vegetable garden. Benjy had to ask him a hundred times just to play catch with him.

"Well," said his father. "First I begged and pleaded and nagged my mother and father. When that didn't work, I got a job cleaning out my grandmother's attic. Took me six months to get that fishing pole."

"He's still working on the red sports car," said Benjy's mother.

Benjy couldn't get a job cleaning out his grandmother's attic. One of his grandmothers didn't have an attic. She lived in an apartment. His other grandmother lived all the way across the country in Oregon. Still, it gave him an idea.

"Could you give me a job?" he asked his mother and father.

His mother looked at him over a spoonful of green Jell-O. It gave her face a funny sickly green look.

"What did you have in mind?" she asked.

Benjy thought fast. "Uh—I could clean out the attic," he said.

She seemed to consider the idea for a minute, then shook her head. "My philosophy about attics is, if it's not bothering us, why should we bother it? So no, thanks."

"I could clean my room," Benjy suggested. "And empty all the wastebaskets."

"You're supposed to do that anyway," said his mother. "Not for pay, just because you're part of the family."

He shouldn't have brought that up.

"I know what," said Benjy. "I could carry in wood for the fireplace. I'm very strong."

"Good idea," agreed his father. "Except for one thing. It's summer. I don't think we'll be needing much wood for the fireplace, not till after baseball season, anyway."

"I guess not," said Benjy. He wasn't having much luck. He thought some more. "How about weeding? I could do the whole vegetable garden for you."

"You could," said his father. "Only oddly enough I like weeding. It gives me a chance to see what's going on in the garden. The thing about doing a job for someone, Benjy, is that you have to offer a service that person is willing to pay for. It has to be something they can't do themselves, or don't like doing. If they don't like doing it, it may be worth it to them to pay someone else to do it."

Benjy nodded. Now they were getting somewhere. All he had to do was find out what his parents didn't like doing.

"Mom," he said. "Out of all the jobs you do every day, is there one that you really don't like doing?"

"One?" Her eyebrows shot up a mile. "You mean I can only pick one?"

This sounded promising. "Pick as many as you want," said Benjy.

She thought a minute. "Changing diapers," she said. "Ironing your father's shirts. And planning meals. I always seem to run out of ideas by the middle of the week."

"Oh," said Benjy. His hopes took a nose dive. Changing diapers was one job he wouldn't take no matter how much anyone paid him. He didn't know how to iron. And as for planning meals, he'd run out of ideas, too, right after hamburgers and hot dogs.

He looked at his father. "How about you, Dad?" he asked.

"Paying bills," said his father right away.

"Oh," said Benjy. Shot down again. Anyone who only had twenty cents in his monkey bank certainly couldn't pay any bills. Plus math was not his best subject in school. It looked like he'd run into another dead end.

He noticed that his mother and father were smiling at each other. Some joke. They must really like to see him suffer.

"There is one other thing," said his mother. "It drives me crazy to try to work on a project in the house with Melissa hanging on to my leg. Tomorrow morning I'd like to paint the bookcase in the playroom. You might be able to help me, Benjy. How would you like a job baby-sitting for about an hour? I'd pay you fifty cents."

"Really?" He looked to make sure she wasn't kidding. Her eyebrows were back where they belonged.

"Really," she said. "It's not big money, but it's a start."

"Great," he said.

"I just thought of one other thing too," said his father. "The car needs washing. But the garden needs weeding too. I won't have time to do both tomorrow. So how would you like a job washing the car? I'll pay you a dollar."

"It's a deal," said Benjy quickly.

All of a sudden things were looking up. He had not only one job, but two. They might be small, but they were real paying jobs.

Benjy did a few fast calculations. Fifty cents from his mother plus a dollar from his father made $1.50. Plus his allowance, which he always got on Sunday, was $2.00. Not bad for one day. Not bad at all.

If only he had a few more days like that, who could tell? Soon he might be making stupendous catches up against the centerfield wall with his Clyde Johnson mitt.

4

»»»»»»»»»»»»»»

"All you have to do is keep her outside," said Benjy's mother. "Play in the backyard or go for a little walk, but stay outside so I can work. Okay, Benjy?"

"Okay," said Benjy.

His mother gave the baby a kiss. "Bye-bye, Melissa."

"Bye-bye," said Benjy's sister with a big smile. When she smiled, her eyes seemed to disappear into her fat face.

"Oh, and if you go near the road, be sure to hold her hand," added his mother.

"Okay," said Benjy.

His sister turned her beaming smile on him. She put her hand into his and led him to the door. "Bye-bye," she said.

"Right," said Benjy. "So long, Mom."

"So long, you two," said his mother.

Benjy let the baby lead him around the side of the house. This was going to be easy. Nothing to it. Why hadn't he thought of baby-sitting before? Maybe he could do it for other people in the neighborhood too. Just in the daytime, of course. He'd call himself Benjy's Baby-sitting Service.

The baby waddled along, smiling and pointing at things. "A-bah!" she said. "Borp!"

Benjy didn't have any idea what she was talking about, but he said, "Right. No doubt about it."

They got to the backyard. The baby stopped walking. She stood there, smiling up at Benjy.

Benjy smiled down at her. Now what? His mother had said they could play in the backyard, but she hadn't said what they could play. What did you play with a baby, anyway?

Benjy looked around for ideas. He spotted his swing, hanging from the apple tree. Of course. Babies always liked to swing.

He walked her over to it. "How about a swing?" he asked.

She didn't look too sure. Maybe she'd never tried it. Well, there was always a first time.

"You're going to like it," he told her. He lifted her up on the seat.

It was kind of wide for her. And she didn't seem to know how to balance. The seat tipped, and she fell off.

It was lucky she was fat. She wasn't hurt at all.

Benjy picked her up. "No, no," he said. "You have to hold on. I'll help you."

He lifted her on again. He put her left hand around one rope. Then he put her right hand around the other rope. It was kind of a big reach. While he was working on the right hand, she let go with the left and fell off again.

Benjy picked her up once more.

"Watch how I do it, Melissa," he said. He sat on the swing, his left hand on the left rope, his right hand on the right rope. "See? It's easy. Now you try."

He lifted her on again. This time she seemed to get the hang of it. She sat there, smiling at him.

"Now I'll push you," he said. "Keep holding on."

He pushed her very, very slowly.

"Moe!" she said. That was one word he understood. It meant "more." He pushed a little harder.

"Wo-wo!" said the baby suddenly, pointing at a squirrel up in the tree.

She fell off again.

Benjy picked her up and brushed her off. It looked like maybe she wasn't ready for swinging.

What else could they play? Benjy tried to remember what he used to do when he was little. It was hard to think that far back.

Ball—that was it. He used to have a big blue rubber ball with red spots on it. His mother or father would roll it to him, and he'd roll it back. That ball was still around somewhere. Benjy went into the shed to look for it.

He found it at the bottom of his box of sports equipment. The spots were all worn off and it was kind of a gray color now. But it was still good for a baby.

"Want to play ball?" he asked her.

His sister smiled and held out her arms.

Benjy rolled the ball to her.

"Yiy-yiy!" squealed the baby as it rolled between her fat legs. She ran after it.

"Now you throw it to me," said Benjy.

She picked up the ball and threw it. Only it landed behind her.

"No, no," said Benjy. "I'm over here."

She picked it up again. She went into a big windup and let it go. This time the ball sailed high in the air, over Benjy's head. Right into his father's vegetable garden.

What an arm! This kid was going to make the major leagues someday for sure.

Benjy tiptoed through the lettuce and got the ball from the middle of the string beans. He checked for damage. A couple of plants seemed a little dented. He straightened them up.

It looked like his sister wasn't ready to play ball yet either. What else was there?

He closed the garden gate and looked to see where she was. She was sitting down at the edge of the patio, playing in some dirt. She wasn't bothering anything, only getting a little dirty. And that didn't matter because she got a bath every day.

Maybe he didn't have to play with her. He could play baseball.

Benjy got his mitt and a tennis ball from the shed. He practiced catching high flies. He got six in a row before he dropped one. And he would have had that one, too, if he'd had his Clyde Johnson mitt.

He checked the baby. She was still playing in the dirt.

He gave himself some harder catches, pretending he was up against the wall in centerfield. He leaped high in the air and caught one backhand, then looked over to see if the baby had noticed.

She was putting a handful of dirt in her mouth.

"No, no, Melissa," said Benjy.

He went over to take it out. But it wasn't dirt. It was ants. She was playing with an ant nest.

"Oh, Melissa—yuck!" He couldn't believe even

a baby could be so dumb. He brushed the ants onto the ground. "Open up," he told her. He looked inside her mouth. He didn't see anything walking around in there. But what if she'd already swallowed some? What if there were ants running around her insides?

It didn't seem to bother her. She was still smiling. He guessed that meant she hadn't swallowed any.

That smile was starting to get on Benjy's nerves.

"I know what," he said. "Let's take a walk. We can go down to the pond and feed the ducks."

Why hadn't he thought of that before? That would keep her out of trouble. And just to make sure, he would watch her like a hawk every minute.

The baby clapped her hands. She loved to feed the ducks.

Benjy couldn't take a chance leaving her alone, so he took her inside with him to get some bread.

"Is that you, Benjy?" called his mother from the playroom.

"Uh-huh," said Benjy. "I'm just getting some bread to feed the ducks."

"Is everything all right?" she asked.

"Terrific," said Benjy.

He got the bread and left. As he passed he looked up at the kitchen clock. He couldn't believe his eyes.

Only twenty minutes had passed. It seemed like twenty hours.

Time sure didn't fly when you were baby-sitting.

The pond was at the end of their road. For Benjy it was nothing to walk there. But for his sister it was a big trip. She didn't seem to mind, though. She trudged along, holding Benjy's hand, pointing at everything they passed. "Bork! Sop!" she said with her famous smile. "Right," said Benjy. "You got it."

She stopped every few steps to look at something—a flower, a bug, a bird in a tree. Benjy had to keep turning her around and heading her in the right direction.

It looked like they might not get there until dinnertime.

It was getting hot too. The baby's face was bright pink.

"Want me to carry you?" he asked.

"Nup," she said.

He didn't know if that was yes or no. He tried to pick her up. She squealed and kicked him.

"I guess not," said Benjy.

At least he could help her cool off. He took off her sundress and carried it. It was all dirty, anyway, and she still had on her diaper.

They kept walking. This was starting to seem like

the longest walk of Benjy's life. But finally he could see the ducks floating in the middle of the pond, three white ones and a brown one. The baby saw them too. "Guck!" she yelled, and she walked a little bit faster.

The ducks came swimming right over. They knew a free handout when they saw one.

Benjy broke up some bread and handed it to his sister. She tossed it into the water with her powerful right arm. The ducks gobbled it down.

"Moe!" she said.

He could see that she didn't need him to help her. He broke up the rest of the bread and handed the whole bag to her.

Benjy sat down on a rock to watch. Another thing he'd have to say about his sister—she sure wasn't afraid. One of the ducks, the greedy big white one, came out of the water. She walked right over and handed him a piece of bread. She was having a terrific time.

Suddenly Benjy saw something move in the water near his rock. It looked like a fish—a big one. Or maybe it could be a snapping turtle, he wasn't sure. He leaned over and watched the spot, waiting for it to move again.

"Moe," said his sister, coming over to the rock.

He kept his eyes on the water. "Shhh," he whispered.

She shoved the empty bag under his nose. "Moe!" she said, louder.

"No moe," he said. "It's all gone. Be quiet, Melissa. I'm looking for a big fish."

She went away, back to the ducks.

Benjy stared into the dark water. It was hard to see anything, the pond was so full of weeds and mud. Out of the corner of his eye he saw something move again. But it was only a dragonfly. The water was quiet once more. It looked like the fish—if it had been a fish—was gone.

He stood up to check on the baby. He didn't see her.

Benjy looked around for the ducks. They were back in the middle of the pond, swimming away. But where was the baby?

For an awful moment Benjy thought maybe she'd fallen into the water. Or been eaten by a duck. That greedy big white one was kind of mean. But knowing his sister, she wouldn't sit quietly by while anything like that happened. She'd yell her head off.

She must have wandered off somewhere to look at something. That was it.

Benjy craned his neck all around. And then he

saw her. She was walking away down the road, her fat little legs working hard. And he knew exactly where she was going. She was going home to get more bread.

He jumped up and started after her. She couldn't walk in the road all by herself. She was supposed to hold his hand. What if a car came? What if his mother saw? She would never let him baby-sit again.

"Melissa!" he yelled.

The baby kept right on walking.

"Melissa, come back here!"

Benjy saw her stop, but it wasn't to come back. It was because her diaper had fallen down. She stepped out of it and kept walking.

This was getting worse and worse. Now she was walking in the middle of the road, past all the neighbors' houses, with no clothes on.

Benjy started running.

The baby looked back and saw him. She must have thought it was some kind of game. She started running too.

She could move fast when she wanted to. Past the Parkinsons' house. Mrs. Parkinson was sitting on her front porch. Past the Boltons'. Mr. Bolton was mowing his front lawn.

Where had all these people come from? None of the neighbors had been outside before.

Melissa kept going. So did Benjy. He was gaining on her. But then he had to stop and pick up her diaper from the middle of the road.

He finally caught up to her at the Rosedales', next door to Benjy's house. She was standing in the middle of Mrs. Rosedale's flower garden.

"Oh, no," groaned Benjy. He had to get her out of there before Mrs. Rosedale saw. Her flower garden was her pride and joy. She didn't let anyone near it.

"Melissa!" he said.

"Farfle?" said Melissa, pointing at a yellow flower.

"No, that's a daisy," said someone.

And Benjy saw it was too late. Mrs. Rosedale had already seen Melissa. She was in the garden, too, on her hands and knees, weeding.

She didn't seem to be angry, though. She was smiling. So, of course, was Melissa.

Benjy knew what Mrs. Rosedale was smiling about.

"Melissa, come out of there," he said.

The baby stopped smiling. She sat down in the middle of Mrs. Rosedale's petunia bed. She had a look that said if he touched her, she was going to scream.

It couldn't be helped. He had to get some clothes on her.

Benjy reached in and picked her up. "Sorry," he said to Mrs. Rosedale.

The baby started to scream.

"That's all right, Benjy," said Mrs. Rosedale, still smiling.

Benjy tried to hide the baby's bare bottom behind him. But she was kicking and yelling. She sounded like a fire alarm.

"Hot day, isn't it?" said Mrs. Rosedale.

Benjy made an attempt at draping the baby's sundress around her, as if she were wearing it. Only she kept wiggling.

"Uh—yeah," said Benjy. "Real hot."

The baby kicked him hard, right in the stomach.

That did it. Benjy got a hammerlock on her and stuffed her under his arm, like a squalling pink baby pig.

"Well," he said, "we've got to go now. So long, Mrs. Rosedale."

"So long, Benjy," said Mrs. Rosedale, going back to her petunias. She still had a smile on her face.

Benjy walked quickly up his driveway. Just as he got to the top he met his mother coming down. "I thought you might like some lunch," she said.

Benjy had never been so glad to see anyone in his life. Without a word he handed her the diaper, the sundress, and the screaming baby.

"What's wrong, Benjy?" asked his mother, looking alarmed. "What happened?"

Never again, Benjy was thinking. This was the end of Benjy's Baby-sitting Service.

"It's a long story," he said.

5

It took him a while to recover. All the time he was eating his peanut butter and jelly sandwich, he thought he'd had it. He was so tired, he'd have to go to bed for the rest of the day. He didn't understand how one little kid could cause so much trouble. Not even a kid—a baby. And she looked so harmless, too, with that big smile.

Benjy watched her smiling as she took apart her peanut butter and jelly sandwich, licked off all the jelly, smeared the peanut butter in her hair, and threw the bread on the floor. Some baby.

But then after lunch his mother went to her purse

and got out three quarters and handed them to him.

Benjy was surprised. "You said fifty cents," he said.

"I know," said his mother. "But I think you deserve a bonus. In the army they call it Hazardous Duty Pay."

Hazardous Duty. That pretty much summed up taking care of his sister. She was a hazard, all right.

"Thanks," Benjy told his mother. He put the money in his pocket and jingled it around. It felt good. All of a sudden he felt good.

"Where's Dad?" he asked. "I'm ready to wash the car."

He found his father in the vegetable garden, admiring his tomatoes. Benjy didn't see what there was to admire. They were about the size of peas, and the same color. But his father was like that about his garden. The appearance of the first baby cucumber was a big event for him. He got all worked up about a perfectly shaped tomato, and if bugs got into the string beans, he took it as a personal insult. His father was what you'd call a serious gardener.

"I'm ready to do the car," Benjy said.

"Great," said his father, pushing back the hat he always wore in the garden. Whenever Benjy saw that hat, he thought of a farmer. Maybe that was what his father should have been. "Hey, Benjy, did you see the size of these tomatoes? That new fertilizer is really working wonders."

"Looks good," said Benjy. "What about the stuff I need for the car?"

"It's all in the driveway," said his father. "And how about all the flowers on the zucchini plants? Looks like we're going to have a bumper crop this year."

Just what they needed, thought Benjy. Last year his mother had fed them zucchini bread and zucchini casserole and zucchini soup and zucchini relish until he thought they would turn green, and they still couldn't use it all up.

"Well, I'm going to get started," said Benjy.

"Fine," said his father. "Don't forget to roll up the windows before you use the hose. And, Benjy—"

"What?" said Benjy.

"Get ready for a treat tonight. Our first string beans of the season!" His father grinned, pulled down his hat, and went back to his tomatoes.

Benjy walked down the driveway.

Everything was there, just like his father said—the car, the hose, a sponge, a bucket of soapy water, and the special cloth his father used for drying and polishing. Benjy had never actually washed the car before, but he'd watched his father do it. All you had to do was squirt the car with the hose, scrub a little with the sponge, rinse it off, and polish. This was an easy way to earn a dollar. He'd be finished in time to go find Jason and play a little baseball.

The first thing to do was roll up the windows. Benjy got in and checked the back ones to make sure they were tight. Then he rolled up the two in front. While he was at it, he thought he might as well see what it was like to sit in the driver's seat. He didn't get to ride in his father's car that much. His father took it to work, so mostly Benjy rode in his mother's rattly old station wagon.

His father's car was nice. It was much smaller than the station wagon, and lower to the ground. It wasn't exactly a sports car, but almost. The seat was made of leather, and the gear shift was on the floor instead of the steering wheel. And the dashboard was crowded with instruments, like an airplane.

Sitting behind the wheel, Benjy could feel what it would be like to drive a racing car, like on *World of Sports* on TV. He saw himself at the starting line, putting on his helmet, checking his instruments. "And in the white car, it's number seventy-seven, Ben Wilkins, starting his first race," said the announcer. A light went on over his head. "Ladies and gentlemen, start your engines!" Benjy turned an imaginary key, and his engine roared into life.

The gun sounded. They were off.

Benjy floored the gas pedal, and his car leaped into the lead. He hunched over the steering wheel, like he'd seen his father do when he was really concentrating on the road. He went into the first turn, taking it easy, saving his power for the finish. But it looked like that snazzy silver car was gaining on him.

He checked the rearview mirror. Yes, it was coming up fast. Benjy moved to the inside of the track and gave his car more gas. He left the silver car in the dust.

Now he was on the last turn, going into the straightaway. And there was a challenge from the black car with the red stripe. It was Mario Pisani, the world champion. He'd never been beaten in this race. This was the crucial moment. Benjy hunched low, whipped the wheel around, and gunned it hard. In the rearview mirror he saw Mario's car skid almost out of control on the turn. It straightened out—but too late. Benjy was across the finish line. He'd won the Indy 500!

Benjy stepped on the brakes, slowing down his powerful engine. He rolled down his window and tipped his helmet to the crowd. The applause was deafening. It wasn't every day a kid came out of nowhere to beat Mario Pisani in the Indy 500.

They wouldn't stop clapping. He had to get out and wave to the crowd.

Benjy stepped out of the car and bowed.

"Woof!" said someone.

Benjy almost jumped out of his skin. Nobody was supposed to be watching him.

"Oh, it's you," he said.

It was Duke, the huge gray dog that belonged to Alex Crowley down the street. He was sitting with his ears perked up, watching Benjy like it was some sort of show.

Benjy looked around quickly to see if Alex was with him. If he was, Benjy was in trouble. Alex would tease him about it for the rest of the summer —and next fall too. He was that kind of kid. The only boy Benjy's age on the whole block, and he had to be a pain in the neck.

But Alex wasn't there. He was away at soccer camp for a whole month, Benjy remembered. Lucky for Benjy.

He closed the car door. "Show's over," he told Duke. "You can go home now."

Duke didn't move. He cocked his head to the side as if he was waiting to see what Benjy would do next.

"Oh, well," said Benjy. "Stay and watch if you want."

He didn't mind. It was kind of nice to have company. Anyway, he had to get started on the car wash. If his father ever got finished in the garden, he might come to see how Benjy was doing. It would be bad if the car was still as dirty as ever.

Benjy turned on the hose. Water came rushing out in a strong, even spray. He aimed it at the car. Water rolled over the hood, splashing off in big droplets. Benjy felt it on his legs, nice and cool. This was fun.

He walked all around the car, spraying. Then he turned off the hose and looked it over.

The car looked cleaner already. This was going to be a cinch. A little scrub, another once-over with the hose, a few swipes of the cloth, and he'd be finished.

Benjy picked up the sponge. "Watch this," he told Duke.

The scrubbing part wasn't as much fun as the spraying. Some of the dirt didn't come off that easily. Benjy's arm got tired. The problem, he decided, was the car being white. Every little bit of dirt showed. When he got his own car, he'd get gray, or maybe brown. That way it would blend with the dirt.

Benjy finished the front bumper and rinsed the sponge. Then he did the hood. He tried switching to the left arm to give his right one a rest. Only his left didn't have as much power. It got tired right away. He switched back to his right.

After the hood he started on the roof. He had to climb up on the hood to reach it. When he got down, he saw he'd left footprints all over the hood. So he had to do it over again.

By the time Benjy got to the back bumper, both arms felt like they were about to fall off. He was hot too. It was a good thing he was washing his father's car, not his mother's. He'd still have half a station wagon to go.

"Finished," Benjy said at last, tossing the sponge in the bucket. Duke waved his tail at him. He was stretched out in the driveway now, panting. He looked as hot as Benjy felt.

That gave Benjy an idea. He went to the faucet and turned it on. But instead of squirting the car, he pointed the hose in the air. The water came down in a fine spray, like a shower. Right away Benjy felt cool, like he'd gone swimming.

"Want some?" he said to Duke. And he gave Duke a shower too.

The dog seemed to like it. He sat with his nose pointed in the air, letting the water drip into his thick fur. And when Benjy stopped, Duke shook himself, giving Benjy another shower.

"Thanks, pal," said Benjy.

Then he turned the hose on the car, rinsing the hood, the roof, the tires. The hard part was over. Now all he had to do was dry it off and he'd be through.

Benjy ran the cloth over the hood, polishing it until it shone. The car was starting to look good. His father would really be happy. Maybe he'd give Benjy a tip for doing such a fabulous job.

He started on the windshield. It was looking good too. No more streaks. Only some of the little drops of water didn't seem to be coming off. What was the matter with his cloth, anyway? Benjy rubbed harder. Then he saw that the drops weren't coming off because they were on the inside.

Benjy shaded his eyes and peered through the windshield. He saw more drops of water, all over the leather seats.

Was it possible he'd left a window open when he sprayed with the hose? But he couldn't have. He'd checked them all before he started.

Benjy jumped down. And there it was. The window on the driver's side—wide open. And he remembered. He'd opened it to wave to the crowd, and then he'd seen Duke and forgotten to close it.

He was afraid to look inside, but he made himself do it. His heart seemed to sink all the way down into his sneakers. There was water everywhere—on the seats, the steering wheel, the instruments, his father's map book that he kept on the dashboard. But worst of all was the floor. It was completely flooded. There must be three or four inches of water there.

What could he do now? If his father saw this, not only wouldn't he pay Benjy for washing the car, he'd yell at him for wrecking it. And his father was likely to come any minute. He had to get rid of that water fast.

The water was so high, it looked as if he could bail it out like a sinking boat. That was it. He'd use the bucket. Benjy emptied it and turned it on its side. He started bailing.

But the bucket was too big for such a little space. It banged into the gas pedal and got stuck on the emergency brake. Benjy needed something smaller, like a tin can. Or better yet, a pump. But if he went to the house to get something, his father or mother would be sure to ask questions.

The only other thing he could use was the sponge. Benjy dipped it into the water and squeezed it out in the driveway. This could take hours. He only had minutes, he was sure, before his father came. But what else could he do?

Dip—squeeze. Dip—squeeze. Benjy checked the level of the water. It looked exactly the same. He had to keep going. Dip—squeeze. Dip—squeeze.

Duke came over to see what was going on.

"Out of the way, boy," Benjy panted. "Got to hurry."

But Duke stuck his head all the way in the door. *Slurrrp*—he took a great big drink of water from the floor.

"Hey, stop that," Benjy said, trying to push him out.

But Duke wasn't a dog you could push around. He was as big as a horse. *Slurrrp*—he lapped up some more water.

Wait a minute, Benjy thought. He stopped pushing. This was it. He had his own pump right here—Duke.

It might not be good for him, all that dirty water. But then again it wasn't that dirty. It came right from the hose. And anyway, Duke drank from the pond and that was pretty muddy. And anyway, Benjy couldn't stop him.

He got out of Duke's way. Three more slurps, and he could see the water level falling. A couple more, and he could make out the floor mat.

Benjy went around and opened the door on the other side.

"Here, Duke," he said.

While Duke worked on the passenger side, Benjy finished the driver's side with his sponge. Then he wiped everything in sight with his cloth—the dashboard, the rearview mirror, the steering wheel.

What if his father came right now? What would he think was going on?

"Hurry, Duke," Benjy urged.

Duke kept slurping. And then finally they were finished.

"We did it!" Benjy said, patting Duke on the head. Duke looked a little full. He went over in the shade of a bush and lay down. Benjy hoped he wasn't going to get sick.

Benjy was just polishing the radio antenna when his father appeared.

"Hey," he said. "It's looking good, Benjy."

"Thanks," said Benjy.

He couldn't believe his luck. He'd finished at just the right second.

Benjy took his father on a tour of the car. The hood, the front bumper, the back bumper, the hubcaps.

"Clean as a whistle," said his father. "I couldn't have done better myself."

Then Benjy opened the front door and showed him the inside.

"Hey, that's a surprise," said his father. "A real bonus. What made you think of doing the inside?"

"Oh, I don't know," said Benjy. "I just wanted to give you my super-duper deluxe cleaning job."

"Well, you sure did," said his father. And he reached into his back pocket and took out a dollar bill. "Thanks, Benjy," he said.

"It was nothing," said Benjy.

6

The next morning Benjy counted his money.

First he poured out everything from his monkey bank onto the bed. It wasn't much. Two nickels, a dime, and a few pennies. Twenty-seven cents altogether. Then he added the allowance his mother had given him yesterday. That made 77¢. He put in his baby-sitting money. He had to get a pencil and paper to add that up. It came to $1.52. He added his carwash money to the pile. That made $2.52.

Two fifty-two. Not bad, considering he'd earned most of it in one day. Next Benjy did some subtraction. At the top of the paper he wrote: "22.95—mitt." And underneath: "$2.52—so far." Then he subtracted. He got $20.43.

"$20.43—to go," he wrote. More than twenty dollars. That was a lot. How in the world was he going to make more than twenty dollars?

"What do you think, Clyde?" Benjy asked.

Clyde was his goldfish. He was named after Clyde Johnson. Benjy liked to talk to him. Not that Clyde ever had anything to say back. Mostly he just swam in circles around and around the bowl or nibbled at the sand on the bottom, looking for lost fish food. It was a pretty boring life being a fish in a bowl, Benjy thought. That was one of the reasons he talked to Clyde. The other reason was that saying things out loud seemed to help him think.

"Twenty dollars is an awful lot," Benjy said to Clyde.

Clyde seemed to agree. He stopped swimming for a minute and looked at Benjy, his mouth opening and closing.

"Do you realize how much baby-sitting for Melissa I'd have to do to make twenty dollars?" He did a little quick arithmetic in his head. "Forty hours, that's how much."

Forty hours with Melissa. That was enough to send a person to the booby hatch. Clyde took a slow turn around the bowl, looking glum.

"On the other hand," said Benjy, tapping his finger on the bowl, "it's only twenty car washes."

Clyde zipped up to the top for a breath of air.

"Twenty car washes," Benjy repeated. "That's not so much really."

The more he thought about it, the more it seemed not much at all. Doing his father's car hadn't been very hard work. If he hadn't left that window open, he could have finished in no time. Of course the scrubbing part was kind of hard, but if he did a few more, he'd toughen up his muscles and it wouldn't bother him. In fact it would be good for him. He could use those muscles for baseball.

"Clyde, old pal," said Benjy, "we're going into the car-wash business."

He got started right away. It didn't take much to go into business. The hose and bucket and sponge and cloth were in the garage. His father wouldn't mind if he used them, he was sure. He'd ask him, but he'd already left for work. All Benjy really needed was a sign.

He went to his desk and got a little piece of paper and his markers. In red letters he wrote: CAR WASH. And underneath, in blue: ONLY $1.00. He thought about it a minute. Then he added: STATION WAGONS —$1.50.

Benjy took the sign and a piece of tape and went downstairs.

His mother was doing the breakfast dishes. Melissa was hanging on to her leg, as usual. Benjy felt sort of sorry for his mother. He could see how hard it would be to get things done that way. It was like trying to swim with an anchor tied to your foot. He didn't feel sorry enough to offer to baby-sit, though.

"Never again"—that was his motto when it came to his sister.

Despite her leg problem his mother was smiling. "What have you got there?" she asked.

Benjy showed her the sign.

"Ah," she said. "Another business venture."

"I need twenty dollars," said Benjy. "That's only twenty cars. Less, if some are station wagons."

His mother nodded. "Well, good luck," she said. "By the way, where are you setting up this business?"

"In the driveway," said Benjy.

"That's what I figured," said his mother. "Well, just keep the hose pointed in the right direction. We wouldn't want to give Mrs. Rosedale any more surprises."

"I will," said Benjy.

He stopped in the garage to take out his car-wash equipment and get a folding chair. Then he walked down to the street.

The mailbox was the best place for his sign, Benjy figured. Anyone going by would be sure to see it. Carefully he taped the sign to the mailbox. Then he unfolded the folding chair and sat down. Now all he had to do was wait for customers.

It was kind of nice sitting there. Not too hot, since

it was a cloudy day. Quiet and peaceful. Maybe a little too peaceful now that he thought about it. He needed traffic if he was going to get customers. But it was early. People were probably still eating breakfast. He would have to wait.

Benjy sat and waited. Everything was quiet. Not a single car went by.

He stood up and looked around. Where was everyone, anyway? They couldn't still be eating breakfast. It was at least ten o'clock.

Was it possible that everyone on the block had suddenly gone on vacation?

Benjy sat down again. He should have brought a book to read. He leaned over and picked up a handful of gravel from the driveway. One pebble at a time he tossed it into the road.

"Hey, what's the idea?"

A blue van with "Frank's Dry Cleaning" written on the side squealed to a stop. A young guy with black curly hair scowled at him.

"Uh—sorry," said Benjy, dropping the pebbles. His first possible customer, and he'd messed it up.

The young guy looked at Benjy's sign. "That's okay, kid," he said. "How's business?" He didn't seem angry anymore.

"I'm just starting," said Benjy. "Would you like a car wash? I can do it for the price of a station wagon."

The guy shook his head. "Sorry, no time. I've got too many deliveries to make. But I can give you some business advice."

"What's that?" asked Benjy.

"Don't throw stones at your customers," he said, grinning.

"Right," said Benjy.

He sat down. The blue van drove off. It went up the Parkinsons' driveway and came down. The driver waved at Benjy as he passed. Benjy waved back.

It got quiet on the street again.

The rest of the morning was like that. Only three cars went by. One was Charlie Fryhoffer's. He'd just gotten his license and a beat-up purple Volkswagen. He drove so fast, he couldn't possibly see the sign. Not that it would have mattered. Charlie washed his car himself, at least once a day. Then there was another delivery van. The driver didn't even glance Benjy's way. And Mrs. Parkinson. She drove so carefully, she didn't look anywhere but straight ahead. Benjy didn't think she saw the sign either.

His stomach started growling. It must be time for

lunch. He untaped his sign and went back to the house.

"Well, how's it going?" asked his mother.

"Not too well," said Benjy. "I think I need a bigger sign."

He didn't want to waste time on lunch. He might miss some customers. He bolted down his peanut butter sandwich so fast that half of it was still stuck to the roof of his mouth when he went upstairs. Quickly he made another sign, on notebook paper, with fatter letters. Then he went back outside.

Traffic seemed to have picked up. Maybe everyone hadn't gone away on vacation after all. Mrs. Bolton went by in her dusty station wagon, her two little kids hanging out the window, waving. Charlie Fryhoffer came home and went out again. So did Mrs. Parkinson. And Charlie Fryhoffer's sister. There must be four cars in that family. You'd think one of them would need washing.

But no one stopped. After a while Benjy got tired of looking up and waving at people as they passed by. Instead he looked down, picking at the fringe of his cutoff shorts.

He'd unraveled them to the point where it was starting to get embarrassing when he heard a bike approaching.

"Hey, Benjy. Want to play ball?"

It was Jason, with his baseball mitt over his handlebars.

"I can't now," said Benjy. "Maybe later."

"How come?" asked Jason.

Benjy pointed to his sign.

"Hey, cool idea," said Jason. "How many customers have you had?"

"None yet," Benjy admitted. "But traffic is getting heavier."

Jason nodded. "I bet you'll get some when people start coming home from work," he said. "Hey, how would you like a business partner?"

Benjy thought about it. It would be nice not to have to sit there all alone. And if they got any customers, Jason would share the scrubbing. But then if he shared the scrubbing, he'd have to share the profits too—fifty–fifty. That meant it would take forty cars to make twenty dollars.

Business might pick up, but it wasn't going to pick up that much.

Regretfully Benjy shook his head. "I can't do it," he said. "I have to make twenty dollars."

Jason whistled. "What for?"

"A new baseball mitt," said Benjy. "The Clyde Johnson model."

"Oh, yeah," said Jason. "I've seen them. They're cool."

He got off his bike. "I'll stay and help you, anyway," he said.

That was a nice thing about Jason. He wasn't piggy. And when you needed him, he stuck around.

Jason leaned his bike against a tree. It was pretty dirty, Benjy noticed.

"Hey, Jason," he said. "How would you like a bike wash?"

"I'd like one," said Jason. "But I can't pay for one. I'm in hock three allowances to my brother for using his barbells."

Jason's brother was a muscle-building freak. He'd been lifting weights since last Christmas. So far he hadn't turned into Mr. Universe, though. He still looked fat to Benjy.

But that gave Benjy an idea. "Got a pencil?" he asked.

Jason dug into his jeans and came up with a chewed-up stub.

Benjy took his sign down. Underneath CAR WASH he added: BIKE WASH—25¢.

"Hey, good idea," said Jason.

They sat down and watched for cars and bikes.

Mrs. Bolton went by again in her dusty wagon.

"She needs you, Benjy," said Jason. "She just doesn't know it."

Charlie Fryhoffer went by again in his purple Volkswagen.

"There's one guy who doesn't need you," said Jason. "Even his rust is shiny. And did you see those windows?"

"That's it," said Benjy. "Windows."

He took the sign down again and wrote: WINDOWS—50¢ EACH.

"That's using the old brain," said Jason.

Benjy taped the sign to the mailbox again.

They sat there a few more minutes. It was getting cloudier, Benjy noticed. He hoped it wasn't going to rain. That would be the end of the car wash for sure.

"Dogs," said Jason all of a sudden.

Why not? You could wash a dog with a hose and bucket as easily as a car. "How much?" Benjy asked Jason, taking down the sign.

"It depends on how big," said Jason. "I'd say twenty-five cents for small, fifty cents for large."

Benjy wrote that down. He could do horses, too, but he didn't think there were any in the neighborhood.

They sat some more. Traffic seemed to have slowed down again. Not a single thing went by, not even Charlie Fryhoffer. He must have run out of gas, thought Benjy.

Benjy felt like *he* was running out of gas. The car-wash business somehow hadn't turned out the way he thought it would. Or the window-wash, bike-wash, dog-wash business. Maybe it hadn't been such a great idea, after all.

"Want to quit and play baseball?" he asked Jason.

Jason looked shocked. "Quit?" he said. "Are you kidding? You've got to get that twenty dollars."

He should have known. Jason never gave up. If he was tied to the railroad tracks with a train coming at sixty miles an hour and only seconds to live, he'd still be figuring a way to chew through the ropes and then derail the train.

"Let me think," said Jason, scratching his head. "Sitting around here waiting for customers isn't working, right? So how about this idea? We go and wash something and then we show it to the owners. When they see how good it looks, they'll have to pay us."

Benjy wasn't so sure. It depended on who the owner was. He didn't think Mrs. Parkinson would like it if they walked up to her house and started washing her windows.

"I don't know," said Benjy doubtfully. "What do you have in mind washing?"

Jason looked up and down the street. The only thing in motion on the whole block was Duke, who was making his afternoon inspection of the neighborhood.

"Him," said Jason.

He gave a loud whistle. Duke came trotting over, waving his tail.

"Good old Dukie-boy," said Jason, patting him like crazy.

"You can't be serious," said Benjy. Jason had nerve, all right. "You know whose dog this is, don't you?"

"Sure," said Jason, grinning. "Old Creepy Crowley. But he's away. He'll never know."

"He'll find out," said Benjy. Alex always found out everything.

"Who cares?" said Jason. "We're doing him a favor. This dog needs us. Look at his fur."

Duke did look sort of mangy. His fur was tangled, like he'd been in the pricker bushes down by the pond. As Benjy watched he scratched himself furiously behind his left ear.

"See?" said Jason. "Probably has fleas too. But don't worry, Duke old buddy. We're going to fix you up. You'll be so beautiful, your family won't recognize you."

Duke wagged his tail. Jason grabbed his collar and led him up the driveway, still talking. "Yes, sir, you're going to feel like a new dog after we give you a nice bath."

Just as Jason said "bath" something seemed to happen to Duke. His tail stopped wagging. And he sat down, right in the middle of the driveway.

"Come on, Duke," said Jason, tugging at his collar.

Duke didn't budge.

"Uh-oh," said Jason. "I think I may have said the wrong thing."

He knelt down in front of Duke and started patting him all over again. "Listen, Duke old pal," he said. "I was only kidding about the b-a-t-h. We're just going for a little walk. You know, look over the neighborhood."

Duke wasn't falling for it. His rear end stayed on the driveway like it was glued there.

"Benjy, come and help me," called Jason.

Benjy didn't have too much hope. If Duke didn't want to move, they weren't going to be able to change his mind. But he tried. "Hey, Duke," he said, giving him a big smile. "Remember the great shower I gave you yesterday? How would you like another one?"

Duke didn't blink an eye or move an inch.

"I'll pull and you push," said Jason. He had that look in his eye again. He'd never give up. He'd stay there all night.

"I think we're wasting our time," said Benjy. But he got behind Duke.

Jason was pulling and Benjy was pushing when all of a sudden Benjy heard a horn beep. He looked down at the road. A gray car was stopped next to the mailbox.

"A customer!" he yelled.

He raced down to the road. It was Mr. Fryhoffer, coming home from work.

"I saw your sign, Benjy," he said. "A car wash is

just what I need. Can't get one at my house now that Charlie has that hot rod of his. Are you still open for business?"

"Sure am," said Benjy. "I wash and scrub and polish and it's only one dollar."

"Sounds good," said Mr. Fryhoffer. "Where do you want the car?"

"Just bring it up the driveway," said Benjy.

He ran back to Jason and Duke. "We have a customer," he told Jason. "You've got to get him out of the way."

"I'm trying," said Jason.

Benjy looked Duke in the eye. "Please move," he said. "Forget the bath. We're not going to give you one, I promise. Just get out of the way."

Mr. Fryhoffer was inching up the driveway. He honked the horn at Duke. Jason was pulling. Benjy was pushing.

Suddenly Benjy felt something splash on his head. It couldn't be. Not now that they finally had a customer. But it was. A big fat raindrop. And then another. And another.

In less than a minute it was pouring. Duke abruptly unstuck himself from the driveway and loped away toward home. Jason raced for his bike. "See ya, Benjy!" he called. Mr. Fryhoffer turned on his windshield wipers and leaned out the window. "Looks like we've been washed out," he said. "We'll make it another day, okay, Benjy?"

"Okay," said Benjy.

He turned and walked slowly up the driveway. The rain was streaming down his face. His hair was in his eyes, and his shirt was stuck to his chest. But he didn't hurry. Who cared if he got wet? What difference did it make? His car wash was washed out.

It was a revolting end to a revolting day.

7

»»»»»»»»»»»»»»

"Hot chocolate?" said his mother. "In the middle of summer?"

Benjy watched the water roll from his hair down his face to his shirt and then drip from his shorts onto the kitchen floor. "Please?" he said.

"Well, all right," said his mother. "But get out of those clothes quick before we have to bail out the kitchen."

When Benjy got back, she was just pouring the hot chocolate into his mug. "One marshmallow or two?" she asked.

"Two," said Benjy.

"Silly question," said his mother, smiling. She sat down across from him at the table. "Well, how did the car-wash business work out?"

"Terrible," said Benjy.

"That bad?" said his mother.

Benjy nodded. It was peaceful sitting in the kitchen drinking hot chocolate with the rain pouring down outside. And with just his mother for a change. Usually his sister was there, too, banging on her tray with her shoe or babbling away in her strange language. It was past time for her to be up from her nap—she must have overslept. Benjy told his mother about sitting by the mailbox for hours while all the cars went by without stopping, and keeping on adding things to his sign, and how when he finally got his first customer, it started to rain.

"That was bad luck about the rain," said his mother.

"It was bad luck about the whole day," said Benjy.

"What do you think went wrong?" asked his mother.

Benjy shrugged. "I guess no one wanted their car washed."

"Well," said his mother, "not enough people, anyway. Remember what your father said? You have to have something to sell that people want to buy." She looked out the window thoughtfully. "One other thing you might keep in mind if you want to be a businessman. People can't buy your service unless they know about it. You have to advertise."

"You mean like on TV and in the newspaper?" said Benjy.

"Not quite like that," said his mother. "But if you just have a sign on the mailbox, only people who happen to pass your mailbox will see it."

"I could make more signs," said Benjy. "And put them up on other roads, like they do for garage sales."

"That's what I mean," said his mother. "Then you can attract customers who don't live on our street."

"I could even put a sign on Route One Seventy-one," said Benjy.

"Well, maybe not there," said his mother. "Cars on the highway are usually going too fast to stop. Anyway, that's a suggestion if you decide to go into business again. It pays to advertise."

"Right," said Benjy.

Benjy didn't go into business again the next day. He thought he needed some time off. Besides, it was still raining.

He fished around under his bed and in his closet and a few other places and found all his baseball cards. Using two shoeboxes, he separated them into this year's and last year's. Then he sorted this year's cards into piles according to teams and put rubber bands around them. That took most of the day. After that he copied Clyde Johnson's picture from last year's card, colored it with his colored pencils, and put it up on his bulletin board.

Looking at the picture made him think about the mitt again. He had to get it, and soon. Otherwise his baseball career would never take off. But he still needed $20.43. How was he ever going to get it?

The next morning Benjy went over to see Jason. He was bound to have some ideas. Not that all of his ideas were terrific, but he always had a lot of them.

"I've got it!" said Jason when he and Benjy were hanging by their knees from the climbing bars of Jason's swing set. "A worm farm!"

"A *worm* farm?" They were looking at the world upside down, with the worms on top. Something must have gotten jumbled inside Jason's brain.

"I'm not kidding," said Jason. "I read about it in a book. This kid digs up his backyard and makes pits and raises worms to sell. And he makes a fortune."

Benjy could just see his mother's face if he told her he was going to have a worm farm. Worms were miniature snakes to her, and snakes made her sick to her stomach. He could also see his father's face if he told him he was going to dig pits in the backyard. This wasn't one of Jason's better ideas.

"It'll never fly," Benjy told him.

Jason let go with his hands and swung so his hair just brushed the ground.

"How about this?" he said, smiling upside down. "We open a gym in my basement, and we charge people to join. Like a health club. And they get to use my brother's barbells and his punching bag and all that stuff."

Too much blood must be rushing to Jason's head.

"Use your brother's stuff?" said Benjy. "Your brother won't even let *you* use his stuff."

"Oh, yeah," said Jason. "I forgot."

Maybe he'd do better right side up. Benjy did a quick skin-the-cat and went to sit in the shade.

Jason flopped down next to him. "Sure is hot," he said.

"The thing of it is," said Benjy, "that you have to have something to sell that people want to buy."

"Right," said Jason.

"If you were a customer, what would you like to buy?" asked Benjy.

"Right now," said Jason, "I'd like to buy a drink."

Benjy looked at him. Jason had done it again. He'd always known he could count on him for ideas.

"That's it," said Benjy.

"It is?" said Jason.

"Sure," said Benjy. "We can sell lemonade."

"Now, that is a good idea," said Jason.

They made six signs on big pieces of cardboard, all with red arrows saying LEMONADE THIS WAY, and put them up on nearby corners. The seventh sign said LEMONADE HERE—15¢ A CUP. They stuck that one on the mailbox. Benjy's mother gave them a pitcher of lemonade and a stack of paper cups. She let them use an old card table for a lemonade stand, and Benjy got two folding chairs from the garage.

He sat down in one—just as Charlie Fryhoffer drove by without even looking.

"Oh, no," groaned Benjy. "This better not be like last time."

But it wasn't. In the first ten minutes three cars stopped. One was Mrs. Bolton with her two little kids and their two friends. She bought five cups. A man from Adams Air Conditioning bought two cups. And another woman in a station wagon with three kids bought four cups. "I saw your sign over on Laurel Lane," she said. "A cup of lemonade hits the spot on a day like this."

As she drove away Jason stuck out his hand. "Congratulations, old pal," he said. "You're going to rake in a fortune."

Benjy grinned. "Same to you. It was your idea."

Money was jingling in his pocket. And the pitcher of lemonade was nearly empty. Already.

Benjy went to the house to get more.

"Already?" said his mother. "Business must be good."

"I'm going to rake in a fortune," he told her.

"In that case," said his mother, "you can pay me back for the lemonade. That's how it's done in business, you know. You have to invest money to make money."

"No problem," said Benjy. "I'll pay you when we close up the stand."

The second pitcher went fast too. And the third. Just about everyone on Benjy's street stopped at the lemonade stand. Mrs. Parkinson and a friend of hers and Mrs. Rosedale and Alex Crowley's mother and sister. And the mailman and the man who came to read the electric meters. And a lot of people Benjy had never seen before.

"Those signs are really working," said Jason.

"It pays to advertise," said Benjy.

His pockets were overflowing with money now. He needed a cash register. When he went to get the fourth pitcher of lemonade, he brought back one of his baseball-card shoeboxes. He dumped all the money into it.

"Wow!" said Jason. "It looks like you get your mitt tomorrow."

"Maybe," said Benjy.

He started counting it. But he'd only gotten to $2.50 when another car stopped, its brakes screeching.

Jason nudged him. "Look who finally decided to give us a break."

Benjy looked up. It was Charlie Fryhoffer.

"You guys got the right idea," he said, whipping out a comb and working over his hair. It was so long, Benjy didn't know how he could see where he was driving. He handed Charlie a cup of lemonade and Charlie drank it in one gulp and held out the cup for a refill. Then he tossed Benjy two quarters. "Keep the change," he said. And he took off down the road, his car clanking like a lawn mower.

"One of these days," said Jason, "his engine's going to fall out right in the middle of the road."

"If he doesn't drive into a tree first," said Benjy.

After Charlie Fryhoffer things quieted down a little. It was getting late in the afternoon and it wasn't as hot. Mrs. Bolton stopped again, but only to ask how they were doing. A man in a tan delivery van stopped and bought one cup. And then no one.

"Want to call it a day?" Jason asked.

"Not yet," said Benjy. "I've got to sell this last pitcher. I'm paying my mother for it."

"How about having a catch while we're waiting?" Jason suggested.

That sounded good to Benjy. He was tired of sitting in the folding chair. His legs felt like they were falling asleep.

Benjy got his mitt and a tennis ball. He let Jason use the old catcher's mitt that used to belong to his father. They took turns pitching a few.

Jason was wild. He walked two batters and then made a wild pitch.

But Benjy struck out the side. His fastball zipped right down the middle, and his change-up got the outside corner of the plate. Even his curve ball seemed to be curving a little.

"Nice throwing," said Jason.

"Thanks," said Benjy. There was a possibility that he might be a pitcher when he grew up instead of an outfielder. If he could just learn to throw a slider.

Then they gave each other high fly balls.

It was the last of the ninth and the Yankees were ahead, 1–0, on a homer by Clyde Johnson. But the Red Sox were threatening. They had two men on and two out and their cleanup hitter, Jim Barker, stepping up to the plate.

He swung on the first pitch. And it was a long fly

ball out to deep centerfield. Clyde Johnson was racing back. Could he get there in time? He was all the way back, up against the centerfield wall. He leaped high in the air.

And he missed. Benjy tripped on a tree root and fell flat on his back. He heard a strange *clunk*. And then he heard Jason laughing.

Benjy looked up. There was the yellow tennis ball, in the pitcher of lemonade.

"Nice catch," said Jason.

"Nice throw," said Benjy. He picked himself up. "Well," he said, "we may as well call it a day."

Jason took the signs down and Benjy put everything away inside. Then they went up to Benjy's room to count the money in the shoebox. It came to $7.30.

"Looks like you don't get your mitt tomorrow," said Jason.

"No," said Benjy. "But at least I'm starting to get someplace."

He handed Jason a dollar.

"What's that for?" asked Jason.

"For helping," said Benjy. "A businessman has to pay his employees, you know."

He went downstairs to find his mother.

SHOES

"How much do I owe you for the lemonade?" he asked.

"Well, it was fifty-nine cents a can and you used four cans," she said. "But I'll throw in the first one free. That comes to—let's see—a dollar seventy-seven."

Benjy counted out the money.

"Thanks," said his mother.

"Thanks for the free can," said Benjy.

He went back upstairs and counted what was left in the shoebox. Now it came to $4.53. Benjy stuffed it all into his monkey bank. Then he got his piece of paper and did some subtraction. Twenty dollars and forty-three cents minus $4.53 was $15.90. He still had $15.90 to go.

Benjy sighed. "Making money sure is tough work," he said to Jason.

Jason was looking through Benjy's baseball cards. "Yeah," he said. "Spending it is a lot easier." Then he looked up. "You know what you've got to do, Benjy? Start thinking big. Forget about stuff like lemonade, fifteen cents a cup. You need to go for big money."

Benjy nodded. That's what he needed, all right. Big money. "But what kind of business can a kid go into to make big money?" he asked.

July already. He would have to come up with an idea himself.

What could he sell for dollars, instead of cents? Something that he wouldn't have to pay for, like he'd had to pay his mother for the lemonade.

The answer popped into Benjy's head like a light bulb going off in a cartoon. A garage sale! Of course. His mother went to them all the time, and sometimes she dragged him along. He'd seen those ladies with their cash drawers piled high with money. You could make big money on a garage sale—real big money. Forty, fifty dollars, maybe even a hundred if you had some good stuff to sell.

He went right to his mother.

She was doing the laundry, with the baby wrapped around her right leg. "Don't tell me," she said. "Let me guess. You've got another idea that's going to rake in a fortune."

"How did you know?" He didn't understand how she could always read his mind.

"There's something about the look in your eye," she said, smiling. "What is it this time?"

Benjy took a deep breath. "A garage sale," he said.

His mother gave him the old raised-eyebrows look. "I don't know," she said. "That sounds like an ambitious project."

"I can do it," said Benjy. "All you have to do is let me use the garage. I'll do everything myself. And I'll clean up afterward too."

Benjy's mother still looked dubious. "What would you sell?" she asked.

"Well," said Benjy, "you know how you're always wanting me to go through my old toys and get rid of the ones I don't play with anymore? I can do that, and sell the stuff I don't want. And I can ask Dad if he wants to get rid of any garden tools or anything like that. And I can sell things for you too."

That ought to get her. She was always complaining that she didn't have room for the things she bought at garage sales. If she'd just get rid of some of her old junk, she'd have plenty of room.

"Hmm," she said, folding a stack of Melissa's tiny shirts and sundresses. "I can't really think of anything I want to sell right now. But you can ask your father."

That must mean she was going to let him do it.

Benjy hit his father as soon as he walked in the door that night.

"Wait a minute," his father protested. "Let me at least put down my briefcase and take off my tie."

Benjy followed him to his study and then up to the bedroom. The second he hung up his tie, Benjy said, "I'm having a garage sale. I'm going to sell some of my old toys, and I could sell things for you too. Have you got anything you want to get rid of, like maybe garden tools or a lawn mower or old furniture or something?"

He really could use some big things. That's what garage sales made big money on.

His father scratched his head. "I don't know, Benjy," he said. "I'd like to help you out, but it seems like I'm using all my garden tools, including the lawn mower. And we're sitting on our old furniture."

His father was just like his mother. He never got rid of anything. No wonder the attic and basement and garage were all stuffed full. It looked like the garage sale was going to be just a toy sale.

It took Benjy two days to get ready for his toy sale.

First he had to go through his toys. That took a whole morning. He found stuff he'd forgotten he had—some good stuff too. It was hard to decide what to sell and what to keep. Babyish puzzles and games could definitely go. But then there were things like his handcuffs. Did he want to sell them or not? He put them in the sale pile on his bed, then took them out, then put them in again. And his stethoscope. It was probably worth a lot, but he liked to listen to his heartbeat every once in a while. He never played with trucks anymore, but what if he wanted to sometime and they were all gone? He decided to sell the broken ones and keep the good metal ones. Then there were his stuffed animals. He didn't sleep with them now, except for his teddy bear, but it was nice to know they were up there on his shelf. He took down the duck that had lost one eye and the monkey with the wire sticking out of his tail and his Raggedy Andy. A few minutes later

he put the monkey and Raggedy Andy back up on the shelf.

Finally his bed was covered with things to sell. Then he had to put prices on everything. That took the whole afternoon. He made the prices pretty high, all more than a dollar except for a few small things like plastic space figures and some rocks from his rock collection. He had to, if he was going to make big money.

The next day Benjy made signs and put them up around the neighborhood. GIANT TOY SALE—TUESDAY, 9–4, they said. After that he set up the sale. His mother said maybe the garage was too crowded to have it there. People might think the storm windows and baby carriage and bicycles were for sale. So Benjy put his stuff out in front of the garage door. He used the picnic table from the back patio and the same old card table and folding chair.

"Good luck," said his father as he backed down the driveway on Tuesday morning. "Hope you rake in a fortune."

His mother must have been talking to him. Why had Benjy ever told her that, anyway?

She and Melissa came out to see the sale.

"Why, Benjy," she said. "It looks terrific. Very professional."

She walked around the picnic table, looking at his price tickets. Suddenly she frowned. "You didn't ask me if you could sell your rocking chair," she said. "That was your father's when he was a little boy."

"It's too small for me," said Benjy. "When I sit down, I get stuck."

"We can save it for when you have a little boy or girl," said his mother.

"Oh, okay," said Benjy.

She picked up the rocking chair, then put it down. "And your grandmother made that picture. You can't sell that."

It was the alphabet, sewn in pink and blue. "But it's too babyish for my room," said Benjy.

"We'll save that for your children too," said his mother.

Now she was walking over to the card table. Benjy held his breath. She picked up the Winnie the Pooh game and the Mickey Mouse game and his blackboard with the magnetic letters and a whole pile of puzzles. "Melissa can use all these things when she's a couple of years older. And she'll definitely want the tricycle."

She was taking away all his big stuff. "But, Mom," Benjy said.

"I'm sorry, Benjy," she said. "But we don't want to have to buy these things all over again in a couple of years. You still have plenty to sell."

He did, but not the stuff he was going to make big money on. He'd put $12 on that rocking chair, and $10 on the tricycle.

She put the tricycle back in the garage, and stacked everything else on the rocking chair. "I'll put these away," she said. "Come, Melissa."

"Bye-bye," said Melissa. She picked up the duck with the missing eye and walked away.

Not her too. He wasn't going to have anything left.

"Hey, that's my duck," said Benjy. He grabbed it away from her. Stuffing started pouring out the eye hole.

"Guck! *My* guck!" shrieked the baby.

Benjy's mother put down the rocking chair and picked up the yelling baby. "On second thought," she said, "I'll put those things away later. So long, Benjy. I'm sure you'll do well on your sale."

Benjy wasn't so sure about that. It didn't seem to be starting too well.

He put the rocking chair inside the garage. Then he gathered up as much stuffing as he could from the driveway and shoved it back inside the duck. He rearranged his display a little. Melissa had switched some of the price tags, he saw. It looked like he was selling his pink rock for $2.50 and his handcuffs for only 25¢.

When everything was back the way it was supposed to be, Benjy sat down to wait for customers. This time he'd come prepared. He had his library book.

He'd almost finished a chapter when three bikes came crunching up the driveway. It was Scott and Kenny and Michael from the next block over. They were all sixth-graders.

"Hi, Benjy," said Scott. "We came to see the giant toys."

"Giant toys?" Benjy didn't know what he was talking about.

"Like you said on your sign. You know, 'Giant Toy Sale.' " Kenny and Michael started laughing.

"Oh, yeah," said Benjy. He laughed too.

They got off their bikes and walked around the tables. Money was jingling in their pockets, Benjy noticed.

"Hey, look at the sick football," said Kenny. Melissa had chewed a hole in one side during her chewing period last fall.

"And the sick tennis racquet," said Michael.

Benjy's mother had gotten it at a garage sale and it had a couple of strings broken.

"You can still throw a spiral with that football," said Benjy.

But Kenny had already put it down. Now he was looking at Benjy's dart board. "Where are the darts?" he asked.

"I lost them," said Benjy. He'd hidden them from Melissa in such a good place that he'd never been able to find them.

"Can't play darts without darts," said Kenny.

"Everything you've got is broken," said Michael.

"Yeah," said Scott. "This sale is just a lot of junk."

That wasn't true. Sure, some of it was a little used. Benjy wouldn't be selling it otherwise. But his space figures weren't broken and neither were his handcuffs or his robot. It just needed batteries. And most of the games had all their pieces. He guessed sixth-graders were too old for all that stuff, though.

They were already on their bikes, heading down the driveway.

"See ya, Benjy," called Scott.

"See you guys," said Benjy.

He opened his book again. He'd only read one more page when someone said, "Ooh! I want the truck!"

"I'll take the handcuffs. And the robot. And the Spiderman car."

It was Mrs. Bolton's two little kids, Adam and Jeremy.

Benjy jumped up and blocked the table so they couldn't grab anything. "You can't play with this stuff," he said. "I'm selling it."

"Oh, boy!" said Adam. He was the oldest. He must be four. "I'm buying the robot."

"I get the truck," said Jeremy. He was about three.

"Have you got any money?" asked Benjy.

Adam felt in all his pockets. "Nope," he said. "But my mom does."

"Well, why don't you guys go home and get some?" Benjy suggested. "I'll save the stuff you want. Get about five or ten dollars, okay?"

"Okay," they said together. They ran down the driveway.

Cynthia Babcock was just coming up. She lived on Laurel Lane and she was in Benjy's class in school. Benjy hated her. She used to chase all the boys and try to kiss them. Now she just thought she knew everything.

"Hi, Benjy," she said. "Are you having a nice summer?"

She sounded like somebody's mother. But she was a customer. You had to be nice to a customer.

"Great," said Benjy.

Cynthia walked around the picnic table, picking things up and putting them down. "Three dollars for the Happy Hippopotamus game?" she said. "That's too expensive. It's only three ninety-eight at the discount store."

"Tell you what," said Benjy. "I'll let you have it for two dollars."

"Oh, I already have it," said Cynthia.

She looked through all the coloring books.

"Batman's partly colored!" she said, frowning.

"Well, sure," said Benjy. "That's why it's only twenty-five cents."

"I'd never buy a coloring book that's been colored," she said.

She told Benjy what was wrong with everything on the table, including his pink rock. "You probably painted it," she said.

"I did not," said Benjy. "I found it in a brook."

"Well, I've got rocks as good as that in my backyard, and they're free," she said.

Benjy could see she wasn't going to buy anything. He sat down and read his book and let her talk to herself. Finally she left.

"Have a nice summer, Benjy," she said.

"Sure," muttered Benjy.

A few minutes later the Bolton boys were back.

"Got the money?" said Benjy.

Adam shook his head. "My mom's not home," he said.

"Who's taking care of you?" asked Benjy.

"A baby-sitter," said Adam. "She won't give us anything."

This was a problem. "Don't you have any money

of your own?" said Benjy. "In your piggy banks or something?"

"I used to," said Adam. "But I spent it for gum."

"I don't have a piggy bank," said Jeremy. "I have a doggy bank."

"Well, go check your doggy bank," said Benjy. "And look around your rooms. See how much money you can find."

"Okay," they said. And they went down the driveway again.

It was almost lunchtime. His mother was going to ask him how he was doing. And so far he hadn't made a single sale. Benjy decided not to have lunch.

Another bike came up the driveway. It was a girl Benjy didn't know. She was around eleven or twelve and she was loaded with money. Benjy could see the dollar bills sticking out of her jeans pocket. But she couldn't make up her mind. She picked up the Happy Hippopotamus game and put it down and picked up the duck with the missing eye and put it down and picked up the tennis racquet.

Benjy asked, "Have you decided?"

"Yes," said the girl. She put down the tennis racquet. "I decided to save my money. My mother's taking me to the shopping center later."

She left, and Adam and Jeremy came back. Jeremy had eleven cents and a piece of gum clutched in his hand.

"That's all?" said Benjy.

"I had a dollar," said Adam. "But I can't find it."

"You can have the gum," said Jeremy.

"Keep looking," said Benjy.

They left, and Sally Spurling came. She was six. She had 58¢ in a purse shaped like a frog. "What can I buy for this much?" she asked.

Benjy pointed out the coloring books and the space figures and the rocks. But Sally kept looking at the handcuffs.

"You don't have enough money for those," Benjy told her.

Sally put her money back in her frog purse and went away, looking sad.

It was beginning to look to Benjy as if he had a problem. The big kids who came to the sale had money, but they didn't want to buy anything. And the little kids wanted to buy things, but they didn't have any money.

He had a feeling he wasn't going to make big money on his toy sale.

On the other hand it would be nice to make something, even if it was small money. Every little bit helped.

He took a marker and started changing his price tickets. He reduced the Happy Hippopotamus game to $1.50 and the handcuffs to $1.00 and the sick tennis racquet to 75¢. He made the coloring books and the rocks two for 25¢. He couldn't go any lower than that. Then he went down to the mailbox and wrote his sign: PRICES SLASHED!

In a few minutes he'd made his first sale. It was the chewed-up football. He sold it to Scott's little brother for 50¢.

Then a girl named Amy bought two coloring books for 25¢.

And Sally Spurling came back. This time she had 83¢ in her frog purse.

"That's still not enough for the handcuffs," said Benjy.

Sally looked sad again. "Do you have a lay-away plan?" she asked.

"Oh, well," said Benjy. "You can have them for eighty-three cents."

He went down to the mailbox again and wrote on his sign: NO REASONABLE OFFER REFUSED.

He sold the pink rock for 7¢ and the Happy Hippopotamus game for 65¢ and the duck with one eye for $1.00. His mother bought that for Melissa when she came out to bring him a sandwich.

"How are you doing?" she asked.

"Not terrific," he said. "But not bad."

By four o'clock Benjy had sold just about everything. Everything but a few of the rocks and the tennis racquet. And he'd made $6.92. It wasn't exactly big money, but it was more than he'd made on his lemonade stand. And that didn't count the money that Adam and Jeremy were still looking for.

"I'll tell you what," he said when they came back for the fourth time, this time with 16¢. I'll help you look."

Benjy closed down his sale and went over to their house.

He shook their banks and crawled under their beds and into their closets and took all the dirty clothes out of the laundry basket so they could look in the pockets. Then they went downstairs to see if any money had fallen out in the dryer.

They found 6¢. That made a grand total of 22¢.

"Is that enough?" asked Jeremy, holding on tightly to the truck. He looked like he might be going to cry.

"We could get a job," said Adam, "and pay you the rest."

Benjy put the 22¢ in his pocket. "It's enough," he said.

Their faces lit up like Christmas trees. They started zooming the truck and the robot around the kitchen floor.

Benjy reached into his pocket and took out the 22¢. "On second thought," he said, handing it back to Adam, "keep it."

Adam looked mixed up. "Keep it?" he said.

"Yeah," said Benjy. "It looks like you guys need it more than I do."

9

»»»»»»»»»»»»»»

The monkey bank was really full now. And it weighed a ton. Besides his garage sale money Benjy had gotten another allowance. There had to be enough money in there to buy the mitt.

Benjy poured it all out on the bed. No wonder it was so heavy. A lot of it was pennies. He counted it. And then he counted it again. It came to $14.47.

Fourteen dollars and forty-seven cents! That was more money than Benjy had ever had in his life. And still it wasn't enough. It wasn't $22.95.

He got his subtraction paper and worked it out. He had $8.48 to go.

Eight and a half more dollars. It seemed like an awful lot to him. "I'm never going to make it," Benjy told Clyde.

Clyde swam perkily around in a circle, swishing his tail. He never seemed to get discouraged.

"I've tried everything," Benjy went on, feeling glum. "Every kind of business a kid can go into, and what do I make? Pennies, that's what."

Clyde opened and closed his mouth. He seemed to be smiling. But that was ridiculous. Goldfish couldn't smile.

"It's all right for you to be happy," Benjy said. "You don't have to work for your fish food."

That was a good point about being a goldfish that he'd never thought of before. It might be a boring life, but it sure was easy. You never had to think if you were a goldfish.

Clyde definitely was smiling. Like he knew he had an easy life.

"So what do you think, Clyde old pal?" Benjy asked. "How do I make eight and a half more dollars?"

But Clyde had no answer. He just turned and swam lazily away.

Benjy had no answer either. He felt like he'd run

out of ideas. And Jason wasn't back yet, so he couldn't go over there and pick his brain. He wouldn't be back until Sunday.

Benjy decided to give himself a vacation. That was what summer was supposed to be for, after all. And all he'd been doing was working. Or straining his brain thinking. He deserved a rest.

For the next couple of days he rode his bike and fooled around with the Bolton kids and rearranged his baseball cards and practiced catching high fly balls in the backyard.

"Would you have a catch with me?" he asked his father on Saturday morning.

"Can't now," said his father. He was on his way out the back door, his farmer's hat on his head and a big smile on his face. "It's harvesttime! Wait till you see what's happening in the garden. It's a zucchini explosion!"

It turned out to be not only a zucchini explosion but a cucumber explosion and a carrot explosion and a string bean explosion. The only vegetable that wasn't ready yet was the tomatoes, and they would be exploding soon. There were tons of green ones.

Benjy's father came back in a few minutes with two baskets full of vegetables.

"How about the size of this one?" he said, holding up a king-size zucchini.

Benjy thought he could probably hit home runs with it.

"Mmmm," said his mother. "Wonderful."

Somehow she didn't sound quite as overjoyed as his father did. Maybe it was because she was the one who was going to get to cook that zucchini into all those breads and casseroles and soups and relishes.

"I wonder what I did with that recipe for a zucchini omelet," she said.

A zucchini *omelet*? Disgusting. Who was going to get to eat all that junk? Who was going to find his plate piled high with vegetables every time he turned around for the next month? Not Melissa. She was too young. It was going to be Benjy.

It occurred to him that this was an emergency.

And right then something clicked inside his vacationing brain. What better way could there be to make money and at the same time get rid of some of those vegetables? He'd open a farm stand.

If his father would let him. He had to be careful how he asked. He wouldn't want his father to think he didn't like his beautiful vegetables.

"Uh, Dad," Benjy said.

"What is it?" asked his father. Now he was lining up cucumbers on the counter. There must be a dozen of them. The kitchen was starting to look like the produce department at the grocery store.

Benjy struggled to say it just right. "Do you think —uh—maybe we might have a few too many vegetables?"

His father frowned. "Too many? Of these beauties? Certainly not."

"I mean," said Benjy quickly, "if there are more than we can eat, and if some of them aren't as good or something, maybe I could sell them. You know, to make money for my mitt."

"Well," said his father, "I guess it's up to your mother. She's the head cook."

Benjy looked at her. She was smiling. "I think we might be able to spare just a few," she said.

So Benjy set up his farm stand. Only this time he didn't use the card table and folding chair. He was getting tired of sitting around waiting for customers to come to him. He decided to take his vegetables to them.

He got out his red wagon. When he was little, his mother used to pull him in it. Now he was the one who did the pulling. He loaded it up with vegetables—a couple of giant zucchinis, some smaller ones, a few cukes, some carrots tied into bunches like they did in the grocery store, and three plastic bags of string beans.

His mother let him take a lot of stuff. Benjy was afraid his father might not like it, but he was back in the garden. "Don't worry," his mother said. "There are a lot more where those came from."

He decided not to bother with signs this time. He'd just take whatever money people gave him.

Benjy started with Mrs. Rosedale. He knocked on her front door. In a minute she opened it.

"Hello there, Benjy," she said. "How are you today?"

"Fine," said Benjy. "I'm selling vegetables." He showed her his wagon. "They're fresh picked from our garden. Would you like any?"

Mrs. Rosedale looked at the wagon. She didn't say yes and she didn't say no. She just started smiling. "Come in for a minute, Benjy," she said. "I want to show you something."

Benjy followed her to the kitchen. And right away he saw why she was smiling. Her kitchen looked just like his kitchen.

There were cucumbers lined up on the counter and carrots in the sink and a few tomatoes on the windowsill.

"Do you have any zucchini?" Benjy asked.

She opened the refrigerator door. The whole refrigerator was stuffed with zucchini.

"I guess you don't want to buy any vegetables," Benjy said.

"I'm afraid not," said Mrs. Rosedale. "But thanks anyway."

He tried the Boltons next. He was pretty sure they

didn't have their own vegetable garden. Mr. Bolton played golf on weekends.

"My, don't those look good," said Mrs. Bolton. "Adam! Jeremy! Come and see what Benjy has in his wagon."

"What's this thing?" asked Adam, picking up a giant zucchini.

"It's a squash," said Benjy.

Adam made a terrible face. "I hate squash," he said.

"Me too," said Jeremy.

"How about some string beans for supper?" asked Mrs. Bolton. "You like those."

"I do not," said Adam. "String beans are yucky."

"So are carrots," said Jeremy.

"I don't even like any vegetables," said Adam.

"You boys don't know what you're missing," said Mrs. Bolton. "I'm going to buy this small squash and a cucumber. Just for Daddy and me. How much do I owe you, Benjy?"

"Whatever you want to give me," said Benjy.

Mrs. Bolton got fifty cents from her purse. "How's that?" she asked.

"Fine," said Benjy. "Thank you."

"Try us again next year," said Mrs. Bolton.

"Maybe these guys will have learned what's good."

"Yuck," said Adam.

Benjy went next door to the Parkinsons'. He knew they didn't have a garden. They couldn't even grow grass in their yard. There were too many trees.

"What a nice idea," said Mrs. Parkinson. "But Mrs. Rosedale brought me some vegetables just yesterday. I'm afraid we can't use any more. There are just the two of us, you know."

The next house was the Crowleys'. Benjy stood back and looked at it. Was that an edge of a garden he could see in back? And was that Alex's sister's bike in the driveway or could it be Alex's? What if he'd come back from camp early?

Benjy decided not to take a chance. He went to the Fryhoffers' instead.

"That's quite a zucchini you've got there," said Mr. Fryhoffer.

"My dad grew it," said Benjy.

"You can tell your dad I think I've got him beat," said Mr. Fryhoffer. "Take a look at this."

He showed Benjy a zucchini as long as his leg.

"I guess you don't want to buy any vegetables," said Benjy.

Mr. Fryhoffer shook his head. "Wait a minute," he said. "Do you have any broccoli?"

"No," said Benjy.

"Well, I don't have any carrots," said Mr. Fryhoffer. "How about a trade?"

Benjy considered. Broccoli wasn't exactly his favorite vegetable. His mother and father liked it, though. "Well," he said, "okay."

Mr. Fryhoffer gave him three huge bunches of broccoli. Plus the leg-size zucchini. "Show that to your father," he said. "Ask him if he can top that."

Benjy piled it into his wagon. This was ridiculous. The wagon was fuller now than it had been when he started. But maybe someone would like to buy some broccoli.

He didn't have any luck at the Dermans'. They got all their vegetables from the Fryhoffers.

There was only one house left on the block. Benjy didn't know the people who lived there. They'd just moved in at the beginning of the summer. If they'd just moved in, though, they couldn't have a garden. It was worth a try.

Benjy rang the doorbell.

A tiny old lady came to the door. This looked promising. She was much too tiny and old to have a garden.

"Mrs. Finelli?" said Benjy. That was the name on the mailbox. "My name is Benjy Wilkins. I live across the street and I'm selling vegetables from our garden."

Mrs. Finelli smiled and nodded. "Come in, come in," she said.

She was going to buy some.

"Right this way," she said. "I'll take you to my husband."

Why was she doing that?

He left the wagon on the front step and followed Mrs. Finelli through the living room and dining room and kitchen to the back door.

"He's right out here," she said.

Benjy stepped out into the most gigantic, most beautiful garden he'd ever seen. It took up the whole backyard. There were row after row of tall bushy plants, like on a farm. There were plants that climbed up on stakes as high as the house. There were plants dripping over fences. Benjy saw zucchini and tomatoes and bush beans and pole beans and green and red peppers and broccoli and cucumbers and melons and even corn. Plus around a hundred other vegetables he'd never seen before. It was like a picture from one of his father's seed catalogs.

"Henry!" called Mrs. Finelli.

A tiny old man stepped out from behind a corn stalk.

"Henry, I want you to meet Benjy Wilkins from across the street," Mrs. Finelli said. "He's a gardener too."

"Well, not exactly," said Benjy. "It's my father."

The old man didn't seem to hear that. He shook Benjy's hand hard. "It's a pleasure to meet another gardener," he said. "Tell me, what do you grow?"

"Oh, nothing much," said Benjy. "Just zucchini and beans and carrots and cucumbers and tomatoes."

The old man smiled. "That's how I began," he said. "Only every year I thought I'd try one new thing. And now look what's happened."

"But how did you grow all this when you just moved in in June?" Benjy asked.

"Ah," said Mr. Finelli. "Well, I had a little help. You see, I am Henry Finelli of Finelli's Garden Center."

Some businessman he was, thought Benjy. He really knew how to pick his customers. Imagine trying to sell vegetables to Henry Finelli of Finelli's Garden Center.

"Would you like to take a look around?" asked Mr. Finelli.

He might as well, thought Benjy. It was the end of his vegetable business.

"Sure," said Benjy.

When Benjy left the Finellis' house, he could hardly pull his wagon. It was overflowing with vegetables. Mr. Finelli had insisted that he take one of just about everything to try. "Who knows?" he said. "Maybe next year your backyard will look like this too."

Benjy's mother met him in the driveway.

"You're losing something," she said.

Benjy looked back. There was a trail of onions and red peppers and green peppers behind him.

"I kind of hate to ask this question," his mother said, looking at the wagon. "But how was business?"

"Well," said Benjy, "I made fifty cents, three bunches of broccoli, a super-giant zucchini, around fifteen onions, a few red and green peppers, one Chinese cabbage, some rhubarb, an eggplant, and a few leeks. The corn is coming next week."

"Quite a haul," said his mother.

Benjy had a sudden thought. "Hey, Mom," he said. "Do you think I could pay for my mitt with vegetables?"

His mother shook her head slowly. "I really kind of doubt it, Benjy," she said.

Benjy started picking up the onions and peppers from the driveway.

"Yeah," he said. "I really kind of doubt it too."

10

“You’ll never guess how many fish I caught,” said Jason.

Benjy didn’t even try. He just waited.

“Twenty-eight,” said Jason. “Bass and sunnies. And you should have seen the one I almost caught. That thing is a monster. It must be twenty-one inches long and it lives under my uncle’s dock. It ate up around fifteen of our worms. Next year we’re going to catch it for sure. We’re going to use a lure. And I learned how to cast and we almost went fishing at five o’clock in the morning in my uncle’s boat but his alarm didn’t go off. So he took us out after dinner instead and he threw out the anchor and it got stuck on some rocks. My uncle had to dive down and cut it loose, only he couldn't find it and we almost had to stay there all night."

"Did you do anything besides fish?" asked Benjy.

"Nope," said Jason. "It was a cool vacation. What's been happening around here?"

"Nothing much," said Benjy. He told Jason about his toy sale and the vegetable emergency and Mr. Finelli.

"Too bad I missed the toy sale," said Jason. "I could have given you some great stuff. All I'd have to do is raid my brother's closet. He's never thrown anything away in his life."

"You're always saying your brother will kill you if you touch his things," said Benjy.

"Yeah," said Jason. "But he wouldn't even notice for about a year. How much did you make?"

"Almost seven dollars," said Benjy. "I could have made more, but I gave some stuff away."

"Not too bad," said Jason. "So now how much do you need?"

"Seven dollars," said Benjy, "and forty-eight cents." He'd counted it again this morning when he put in the fifty cents from Mrs. Bolton and his allowance.

"Seven dollars and forty-eight cents," repeated Jason. "That's not so much. You're really getting there, Benjy. Let me think about this."

Benjy was glad to let him. His own brain was worn out from thinking about it. He lay on Jason's top bunk and stared at the ceiling, thinking about nothing at all.

"If only I hadn't eaten all those fish I caught," said Jason, "we could sell them."

"You ate twenty-eight fish?" Benjy said.

"Well," said Jason, "some of them were kind of small."

Benjy was getting tired of looking at the ceiling. He glanced over at Jason's poster of Tony Trumbull charging through the line of scrimmage. There was no getting away from it—football season was almost here. He looked back at the ceiling.

"Worms," said Jason suddenly. "That's it! We can sell worms. Hey, Benjy, we'll rake in a fortune! Do you know how much they charge for night crawlers at the lake? A dollar fifty for this teeny little carton. And we can get them free in your father's compost pile."

Benjy could feel Jason bouncing up and down on the bed underneath him. "Wait a minute," Benjy said. "Hold everything." Jason's brain must still be